First Helping

Stan's family were
having breakfast.

Food was one of Stan's favourite things.
If he stayed nearby, Stan knew he might
get some, too.

The one Stan called Crumble always
dropped crumbs on the floor.

The one Stan called Handout always gave
him a handout.

Stan got a special surprise when the one he called Bigbelly dropped a cereal packet on the floor.

Oops!

Wow! It's raining snacks!

The one Stan called Canopener was
furious. She was the one who usually
prepared Stan's meals.

Canopener chased Stan into his bed.

Stan lay down and heaved a big sigh.
He heard Canopener and Bigbelly talking
about him.

A little later, Stan heard Handout and Crumble talking about him.

9

Stan listened to Canopener's plan.

Second Helping

Bigbelly and Stan
set out on their
walk. They went
along the path
by the canal.

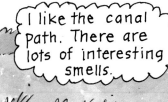

I like the canal
path. There are
lots of interesting
smells.

After a bit, Bigbelly
stopped. He took a
rug out of his bag.

Bigbelly made himself comfy on the bank
of the canal.

Then he took something else out of his
bag.

Bigbelly threw the ball and
Stan went bouding after it.
He was back in a minute.

Bigbelly threw the ball again … and
again … and again.

Stan was enjoying himself, unlike Bigbelly.

Stan ran up and down the canal path for ages.

At last, he noticed a drainpipe.

The field was full of piles of hay, but there was no sign of the ball.

Stan sniffed every pile until…

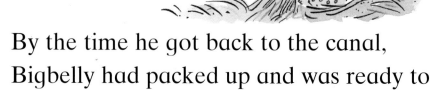

By the time he got back to the canal, Bigbelly had packed up and was ready to go home.

Third Helping

In the afternoon, it was Handout's turn to take Stan for a walk. Handout had arranged to meet his pal Emmo in the lane. They waited there for ages…

At last, Handout jumped off the wall.

They went to the football pitches, where they found Emmo having a kickabout.

The boys began to play, and Stan tried to join in.

Stan had to sit and watch.

Stan ran back towards the lane.

Stan picked up the jacket and headed back towards the football pitches.

However, when he turned out of the lane…

Stan saw Scott and Sprinter heading towards him.

There was a plank lying at the edge of a building site.

However, the plank was lying on a barrel. It was very wobbly and it tipped up.

Stan slid and landed, face first, in a muddy puddle just as Sprinter passed by.

Stan tried another escape
route. He found a wall
which was low enough
to climb over.

He climbed up
a shed roof and
down the
other side.

But he got stuck at the wrong moment.

First swimming, now
flying! Are you a fish,
a bird or a dog?

Stan arrived back at
the football pitches
just as Handout and
Emmo were saying
goodbye. Handout
didn't even notice
that Stan had been
away.

Fourth Helping

The next morning, Canopener opened
a can and gave Stan his breakfast.

> Huh! I'm sure there's less food here than yesterday.

When he'd eaten, Canopener and
Crumble took Stan to the park.

> She doesn't stand any nonsense. I'll get a proper walk now.

They walked along the busy high street
and stopped at the new crossing.

 They crossed when the
green light came on.

At the park they headed for the pond where Canopener tied Stan to a nearby bench.

Then Canopener took Crumble to feed the ducks.

The wind caught Crumble's empty bag and blew it out of her hand. It landed near Stan.

He pulled on the lead so hard, the knot came undone. He chased the bag as it floated away again.

Stan caught up with the bag and licked a few crumbs from the inside. When Canopener arrived, she told him off.

To make matters worse, Sprinter had watched the whole event.

It was a bad end to another bad walk.

Fifth Helping

The next day, one of Canopener's friends popped in to see them.

Stan called the lady Friendly. She was a dog trainer but she always spoke kindly to him and Stan knew she kept dog biscuits in her pocket.

Canopener appeared with the tea and they sat down on the sofa.

33

When she had finished her tea, Friendly said goodbye.

Stan ran through to the sitting room. He jumped up on the sofa to watch Friendly go down the street.

After that, everyone wanted to meet
Superdog Stan.

Stan was surprised when Sprinter came
over to congratulate him.

Canopener took a scarf from her pocket to use as a lead. Then Stan led his family home at great speed.